Andrew J. Rogers

The Great Falls of the Potomac River of Virginia

with its resources and outlets, as the manufacturing center of the United

States

Andrew J. Rogers

The Great Falls of the Potomac River of Virginia
with its resources and outlets, as the manufacturing center of the United States

ISBN/EAN: 9783337239077

Printed in Europe, USA, Canada, Australia, Japan

Cover: Foto ©Andreas Hilbeck / pixelio.de

More available books at **www.hansebooks.com**

THE

GREAT FALLS

OF THE

POTOMAC RIVER OF VIRGINIA,

WITH ITS

RESOURCES AND OUTLETS

AS THE

MANUFACTURING CENTER OF THE UNITED STATES.

ANDREW J. ROGERS.
WASHINGTON, D. C.

WASHINGTON, D. C:
CHRONICLE PUBLISHING COMPANY, 511 NINTH STREET.
1873.

THE

GREAT FALLS OF THE POTOMAC RIVER

AS A

MANUFACTURING CENTER.

It is generally conceded that the Great Falls of the Potomac river is the greatest available water power in the United States; and the abundant mineral, agricultural, commercial, and other natural and artificial resources necessary to manufacturing purposes, renders it a most desirable base for the great manufacturing centre of our country. It is situated fourteen miles above the city of Washington, and elevated about 158 feet above the height of the inflowing tide at Georgetown. And in this continued declivity there can be secured, at the several available points, ample power for the most extensive manufactories. But the greatest amount of this power is concentrated at the Great Falls where the river is nearly half a mile wide, and is divided by a chain of islands located near its centre, thereby giving two currents, respectively known as the Virginia and Maryland channels—the Virginia being now the main stream. At this point, within the limits of the property owned by the "Great Falls Manufacturing Company of Virginia," we have about 85 feet available fall with a flow of 2,100 cubic feet per second, which, uninterrupted, is equal to 13,000 horse power, and sufficient to run 20,000 looms, aggregating 900,000 spindles, together with the necessary machinery for divers other branches of manufactures which can be carried on by the conjointed use of the same power without impairing the force requisite to cotton spinning and the like. But in order to supply the cities of Georgetown and Washington with water, the United States has constructed a dam so penetrating the Maryland channel as to turn about one-eighteenth part of this flow through the conduit for that purpose. This calculation is based upon the flow during the dry season, which never exceeds three months in the year, and applies especially to the volume of water flowing at the Great Falls, and shows what amount of power may be safely relied on thereat for cotton spining and the like, which usually requires power every day alike throughout the year. From the 1st of September to the 1st of June the flow is thought incalculable, and is so confined within the banks of the river as to furnish an inexhaustible power ; and our climate is such that we can continue operations throughout the entire year.

So abundant is our supply of granite and other imperishable building stone that the scientific enterprising engineer, who shall be provided with the necessary capital, will find little difficulty in constructing imperishable water basins, channels and races adequate to the perpetual conversion of this entire power to use at command. And as there is a continuous declivity of over 250 feet from Harper's Ferry down to the Great Falls, it is possible, and will doubtless prove profitable to fit up one or more immense basins or reservoirs in some one or more of the valleys above, wherein a sufficiency of the surplus flow during the more aquarius seasons may be turned and so converted as to double the power throughout the dry seasons, thereby perpetuating all necessary power the year round for all time.

As we improve this water power and begin concentrating manufactories thereat, steam power will, of course, be brought to coöperate in more general productions. The manufacture of pig-iron, as well as steam-carriage rails, machinery, fire-arms, and all kinds of metal instruments, must necessarily follow the adequate development of the Great Falls, since it is in the midst of, and in communication with, inexhaustible fields of superior qualities of ore, and a superabundance of the best qualities of smelting coal—all easy of access.

In the increasing demand for better railway tracks the observant mind cannot fail to see a very large, important, and lucrative business in the manufacture of a continuous rail, comparatively without joints, by virtue of its tubulous intersections, which secures to the traveler and live stock *in transitu*, not only ease, comfort, and safety, but double the speed afforded by the present system of rails, from which, it is safe to state, that seven-tenths of the railroad accidents occur. And surrounded as we are by iron and coal, and open to, and in communication, either by water or rail, with the divers railroad lines, throughout the country, we feel safe in predicting that an extensive branch of *this* manufacture will, at no distant day, be established at the Great Falls. But the chief staples for manufactures at this point is cotton, wool, and wood. And, as will be seen within the following pages, we have the most direct and unbroken lines of easy and cheap transportation, both by water and rail, from the vast cotton fields of the South, whereby the raw material can be placed at our factories at much less cost than at any other important manufacturing point, and in fact, about as cheap as it can be placed at New Orleans.

With regard to wool it may be correctly stated that both the Virginias are most admirably naturally adopted to the growing of this very indispensible article. In fact, it is conceded by all who are well informed on the subject, that for wool-growing the Virginias are equal to, if they do not excel, all other sections within our reach. And there is no portion of these States more suitable for sheep-raising than that surrounding the Great Falls. Nature supplies the forage in the wild uncultivated state, leaving the shepherd only to guard his flocks and gather in his wool at comparatively little cost. Wool-growing is daily becoming more important, and hence, rapidly increasing in the Virginias.

Ample quantities of wood for cabinet and all kinds of manufacture from this material abound at and about this point, and conveniently along the several lines of transportation. So, also, heavier timber, not only for home consumption, but for abundantly supplying foreign markets. Though there is now but little production of hemp, flax, &c., there is no reason why it should not become an important staple of manufacture at this point.

Wheat, as a matter of course, is to become one of our great staples of manufacture from the fact that we are surrounded by some of the most fertile wheat-growing sections, and by railways directly in communication with others equally productive.

On the Virginia side of the Potomac, adjacent to the Great Falls, we have one of the most picturesque sites, with all necessary conveniances for founding, and material for building, a large and prosperous city. And as every water-power developed and practically employed in manufacturing necessarily founds, builds, and populates a city adjacent thereto, we may safely assert that a flourishing city will speedily follow the adequate development of this great and advantageously-located water power. In fact, it has been laid down as a safe proposition that a population of 1,000 will accrue to every 166 horse-power actually employed in textile or equivalent manufactures.

The Merimac Falls, at Lowell, Mass., has about 9,000 horse-power; and by its development we find 40,928 population, annually yielding a value of $24,000,000 in manufactures; and this population, with its enterprises, increasing at about the rate of ten per centum per annum. Lawrence, much younger than Lowell, and with less power, has already a population of 30,000, with a corresponding annual valuation. Fall River, with only 1,600 horse-power, and which, in 1860, had only a population of 14,026, numbered at the last canvass 26,766, with an annual valuation of $17,000,000. Within the last few years steam-power has been brought into coöperative use at this place, which, of course, gives a greater impetus to the growth of this thriving locality.

The Androscoggin Mills at Lewiston, Me., which commenced operations in 1860 with $1,000,000 capital stock, under the management of Amos D. Lockwood, Esq., having 800 horse-power, running two mills with five (Turbine) water wheels, 1,100 looms, aggregating 50,000 spindles, employs, in manufacturing cotton, 788 females and 312 males; and, though more or less impeded through the dry and frozen seasons, annually produces 6,500,000 yards of cloth and 1,800,000 grain bags, besides other productions.

The Great Falls Manufacturing Company of Virginia, which organization exists by virtue of valid charters from both the States of Virginia and Maryland, now own the Great Falls water-power of the Potomac. And, in addition to this power, the company owns about 900 acres of land adjoining thereto on the Virginia side, together with the islands between the channels, and the land privileges along the waters' edge on the Maryland side of the river. The charters provide that, for city and other purposes, the company have the right to acquire, own, and control 2,000 acres more on the Maryland side, and 3,000 acres more on the Virginia side of the Potomac, adjoining their present property. And the charters also provide for developing the water-powers for manufacturing purposes, the founding and building the city, and bridging the Potomac thereat.

There is also a canal (belonging to the company) over one mile in length, leading out of, and along the line of the river, through the lands of the company, and emptying back into the river below the Great Falls, which was dug out and built up years ago, and, with repairs, will prove valuable for milling purposes.

The 900 acres now owned by the company, as well as that adjoining and to be acquired, lies well for the base of a city. And after appropriating about 200 acres thereof, along the line of the river, as will best suit for mill purposes, we propose laying out the remaining 700 acres with such other as may be found necessary, and proceed to build a city upon the most improved plan, guaranteeing health, convenience and beauty. And to this end it is suggested that the streets shall square with the four points of the compass. Those running east and west to be 100 feet wide, reserving twenty feet on either side for parking in front of the houses, and leaving ten feet for sidewalk and forty feet for roadway. The cross streets running north and south to be sixty feet wide, reserving ten feet on either side for sidewalks, and forty feet for roadway. Each square fronting 600 feet on the streets running east and west, and about 300 feet on the cross streets, reserving fifteen feet for alleys through the centre of each square, from east to west and north to south. The lots fronting on the east and west streets to be 25 by 135 feet, exclusive of the reservation for parks in front; and the owners of each lot to keep their respective park-front set in green turf, growing shrubbery, &c.

By some such plan the 700 acres alone will furnish about 125 squares of 48 lots each, aggregating about 600 building lots, (making due allowance for waste ground,) which, at $100 per lot, would give us $600,000. This will suffice to show what may be realized by a judicious disposition of the ground, whatever may be the plan adopted.

In regard to building and other material, ample supplies of superb marble and granite, and choice seneca or sand, blue, and other building and paving stone, as well as brick and fire-clay and cement abound at and within the vicinity of the Great Falls. And, as has been previously remarked, at and around the Great Falls, and along the lines of the canal and converging railways there is no lack of choice wood and timber of various kinds, not only for all needful purposes in home consumption, but for other American as well as foreign markets. Gold has been discovered to exist at this point, but, as yet, not sufficient to authorize working some of the veins. The soil, not only around this point but more or less throughout the States of Virginia and Maryland, abound in mica, silica, alumni, "terra cotta," concrete, soap-stone, blue and potter's clay, and divers elements of earthenware and glass, and other productions necessary to private and public improvements.

There will be no lack of skilled and unskilled labor for every grade and class of work to be performed, save in regard to cotton-spinning, weaving, &c. This, however, can be easily supplied by emigrating a few skilled hands from New England or Great Britain, from whom our people can soon acquire the requisite skill. And it is certain that when the present, or any other company, composed of people capacitated, and who will manifest an earnest determination to develope and convert this power to manufacturing, their capital stock will be most liberally taken. In fact, the combined good will and zealous coöperation of this entire section will be most substantially given.

THE REASON WHY

this great water-power has so long remained undeveloped has been mainly owing to the adverse influences of the institution of slavery. The people of the slave States, owing to their peculiar callings and business and social education, lacked the requisite practical genius to such development : and as they found it difficult to procure it, save in the brain of the Abolitionist—the avowed vigilent foe of chattel slavery—they preferred to let their water-powers run waste and ship their cotton and wool to New England and Great Britain for manufacture.

Years ago, prior to the development of the falls of the Merrimac river, from which grew up the city of Lowell, the same parties who inaugurated that enterprise offered $300,000 for the Great Falls water-power of the Potomac, but the owners refused to sell at any price. These owners eventually died, and the property changed hands, and was finally offered for improvement; whereupon, just prior to the late war, a company was duly organized, but failed to get under way before the war frustrated their plans.

The adverse effects of slavery has gone with the ill-fated institution, never more to disturb the march of industrial and intellectual progress. And now this invaluable property is again offered, with largely increased advantages, for development and practical use.

In regard to

this vicinity, and, in fact, more or less of the entire States of the Virginias and Maryland are open to, and anxious for, industrial emigrants from any and all portions of the civilized world. Fertile lands can be secured very cheap and on the most favorable terms, and in quantities to suit almost any class of emigrants.

The old prejudices growing out of the elements of slavery, and which more bitterly operated immediately after the war, having irrecoverably lost their animosity, are necessarily giving place to the reciprocal relations which tend to the recognition of the common brotherhood of man. This is not only natural in the order of intellectual progress, but the legitimate work of self-interest, which is ever the prime actuator of mankind in the corresponding relations of society. While we sustained and cherished slavery it was to our interest to shut out any and all influences likely to impair our legal rights therein. But now that this institution is forever happily gone from our country, and its hitherto retarding influences are fast dying out, we find it absolutely to our interest to court the emigration of the enterprising industrial classes from any and all sections.

With regard to the city of Washington, which must always sustain a very important relation to our new rival city soon to loom up at the Great Falls, the "Report of the Joint Committee on Manufactures of the Legislative Assembly of the District of Columbia," published June 11, 1872, from which we quote freely, calls attention to the well-known fact that Washington and her adjoining sister city, Georgetown, are situated at the head of ship navigation on the Potomac, only eighty miles from Chesapeake bay, and but one hundred and forty-five miles from the Atlantic, by a channel open at all seasons of the year, through which ships of at least nineteen feet draught of water can come to the wharves at Washington, and those of the largest tonnage to the wharves at Alexandria, only four miles away from our docks, and adds, that slight dredging of the channel between Georgetown, Washington, and Alexandria would afford a depth of water easily and cheaply maintained for all vessels that might, by any possibility, be needed for our commerce or other purposes. During the late war, fleets of vessels of the largest size lay in the secure anchorage of the Alexandria portion of our harbor, and, in fact, at the wharves. Vessels of war of more than 2,000 tons now pass to the navy-yard adjoining the city of Washington. So that a very inconsiderable expense would bring like-sized vessels to our wharves along our Washington river front.

It is thus evident that by our merely natural facilities we are at once in easy and immediate communication with every seaport town along our wide-extended coast, and can readily enter upon any scheme of commerce that the world may offer. Our ships and steamers can pass as swiftly and safely from this port as from Philadelphia or Baltimore, and both of these great commercial marts have in other days had a commerce that extended to the Indies and China, and "the uttermost parts of the earth." And though our harbor is one of the best on the Atlantic slope there are measures now on foot, with the appropriations, for making it commensurate with the most extensive shipping and general commercial interest.

But however admissable the port and its ready facilities for maritime commerce, it is quite certain that this alone will not build up a great city. It is an important element in our success as affording an easy and available water-carriage to the world—always the cheapest method of transportation. But let us also consider the artificial means, such as canals and railroads, for commerce and manufacturing industry. Among the first is the

which runs *via* the Great Falls. Beyond all advantage there is to commerce and trade in this water-way, it has a peculiar interest in this, that it was the legitimate outgrowth of the efforts and work of Washington. From earliest manhood, in 1753, he was impressed with the necessity of water communication between the tide water of the Potomac and the great western rivers, and later in life he urged the development of plans having this end in view, as a matter of national concern, being deeply impressed with the wisdom of the policy of connecting the East with the West by a public highway, of which this water communication was to be the introduction. His plan contemplated the improvement of the Potomac navigation to Fort Cumberland, or the highest practicable point, thence to reach, by portage or roadway, the nearest tributaries of the Ohio. This grand plan was afterwards brought more fully to realization in this canal, which was begun in 1828, under and by virtue of statutory enactments in Virginia, Maryland and the Congress of the United States. Though it has opened up the way of traffic and trade from a portion of Virginia and Maryland, and is the graat course for bringing the vast quantities of coal from the Cumberland mines, it is not yet the advantage to our city that it will be when the new plans we hope to see adopted are in full vigor of prosecution. After the completion of this canal to Cumberland, the Baltimore and Ohio railroad was opened to the towns of the Ohio river. It was thought then that there would be no need of extending the canal further. But experience has proved that water-carriage for long distances is cheapest, whether on rivers, as the Mississippi or the Ohio, or on canals, as the Erie in New York.

As now built and used the Chesapeake and Ohio canal from Georgetown to Cumberland, Maryland, is 184½ miles in length, width fifty feet, depth six feet, with a total fall of 606 feet, and has cost $10,506,309. But the day of canals, in its true meaning, is to come again, and all that Washington hoped, prophesied, or worked for, is yet to come true, because the inevitable law of demand will render a wide, safe, and cheap water-way to the great rivers of the West absolutely necessary. Development of the adjoining States has scarcely begun, while the far West, with their great products, must also join in the demand for easy, cheap, and direct communication with the Atlantic coast. The commerce of West Virginia and Eastern Kentucky and Tennessee absolutely languishes for this very lack of facility to place their products in market. Our railroads answer all these purposes very well, but, in the nature of things, they cannot supersede the canal. We, therefore, call the public attention to the old arguments, so often urged in 1784, and thence forward, as being vastly more important now than then. We call attention to the great Erie canal, with all the disadvantages of months of stoppage every winter on account of ice, a deadlock that would hardly interrupt the continual use of a water-way in this latitude. And, eventually, the Chesapeake and Ohio canal will be extended to the navigable waters of the Ohio river.

From a condensed statement, now before us, showing the increasing business and financial condition of the Chesapeake and Ohio Canal Company, it appears that the net revenue for 1871 exceeded that of the preceding season $197,186 54.

The expenses of 1871, as compared with 1870, show a decrease of $47,134 45.

Though we have not the exact figures for 1872 before us, we are enabled to state that the net revenue shows a prosperous increase, with a corresponding decrease of the expenses. In fact the business of this canal has so largely increased that the company is adopting every means for equally increasing its facilities; and when the Great Falls shall have been developed, which it is now manifestly clear will be done at no distant day, this water-route will be deepened and widened commensurate with the demands for transportation between Washington and this inevitably-to-be *manufacturing center.*

STEAM-PACKET LINES, ETC.

Our several steam-packet lines, and other water crafts, which relatively apply the same to the Great Falls as they do to Washington, furnishes safe, accommodating and cheap transportation between this point and Boston, New York, Philadelphia, Baltimore, and Norfolk, and *via* Norfolk and Acquia Creek (and thence *via* rail) with Richmond and other points along the Atlantic coast.

The principal article of export by steam-packets and other water craft is flour, of which as much as 98,638 barrels have been shipped in one year. In 1871-'72 a new and increasing article of commerce (sumac) has been largely shipped by this line from Virginia—in fact as much as eighty tons per annum having been forwarded within the past two years. With the increase of domestic enterprise there is every reason to believe that these exportations will be enormously increased.

We may remark here that the value of the flour production of the District for 1871 amounted to $2,000,000, and the amount of wheat represented in this supply was about 787,000 bushels. In 1872 the value of the exportation of this product was about $3,000,000. It may also be stated that the lumber traffic is by no means inconsiderable. During the years 1871 and 1872 over 25,620,000 feet were brought hither in schooners. The value of this trade for those years was over $700,000, and this year a very large increase is anticipated. This fact of itself shows how great a field is open for the manufacture of lumber in the forests available in our more immediate neighborhood.

RAILROADS.

Until lately our railroad system has been somewhat inefficient, there being but one, and that a branch line. *via* Baltimore, by which we could claim a connection with the North and East, and, indirectly, with the West; and only one line, the Orange and Alexandria, connecting us with the South. But now several new roads have converged, and are still converging at and passing through, and others starting from Washington, rapidly putting us in direct and easy communication with all the agricultural, mineral, and commercial sections.

By way of the Washington and Alexandria branch road, which connects us with the Orange and Alexandria railway, we are connected with the Alexandria and Manassas Gap, and the Loudon and Hampshire roads, both of which extend through richly fertile sections of the Old Dominion.

The Baltimore and Potomac Railroad Company has constructed a line of railway, under charter granted by the State of Maryland and the Congress of the United States, extending from the line of the Northern Central railway, on the east side of the city of Baltimore, to the city of Washington and across the Potomac river to the Virginia shore; also to a point twenty-four miles south of Baltimore, through the lower counties of Maryland to the Potomac river, at the mouth of Pope's Creek. The line secures a direct railroad connection for railway carriages through the Northern Central railway, with the vast system of roads west, northwest, and to the Pacific, controlled by the Pennsylvania Railroad Company, and by its Northern Central connections with the great coal, iron, and lumber regions of Pennsylvania, the western sections of New York, and the lakes, and the dominion of Canada; also by the Union Railroad of Baltimore an uninterrupted connection for locomotive engines, with the system of roads to Philadelphia, New York, and the whole eastern section of our country.

By the reconstruction of the Long bridge across the Potomac for railway purposes at Washington, and the construction of the Alexandria and Fredericksburg railroad to a connection with the Richmond, Fredericksburg, and Potomac railroad, an uninterrupted connection is secured with the system of Southern railroads converging at Richmond, Virginia. Washington, by way of the Baltimore and Potomac, secures a competing line to all sections of our vast country, and this, with unbroken connections, upon which passengers and freight can be moved by steam without transfer or break of bulk, to all other sections of the country. And especially by this line, with its divers tributaries converging at Richmond, together with the Orange and Alexandria railway, which is connected, *via* railway from Charlottesville to Lynchburg, with the Virginia and Tennessee railroad, we have direct and unbroken lines to the vast cotton, rice, sugar, tobacco, and other productive fields of the South and Southwest.

The line has been built, as we learn, in the best manner and at great cost; the work in Washington costing about a million of dollars, and the tunnel under Baltimore nearly two millions.

The projectors of this enterprise expect to draw to it a
2 G F

large and growing trade, owing to the perfect connections
it secures with the great Pennsylvania trunk lines of railways to all western points, by the Northern Central and
Philadelphia and Erie, with Buffalo, Niagara Falls, the
lakes and Canada, and the great coal, iron, and lumber
regions of Pennsylvania. By connections with the Southern system of roads, south of Richmond, an outlet by rail
will be afforded for the great staple productions of that
section of the country. The amount of coal seeking
Washington by this road will reach at least 100,000 tons,
and, with the growth of the city, and the improvement of
the Great Falls, it will rapidly increase Our people will
henceforth be enabled to get this staple article every day
in the year, in cars loaded directly at the mines.

The connections with fast express trains, with palace
and sleeping cars, running through to the North and West
and South, with ample accommodations for local traffic,
will doubtless secure to the enterprise a large and increasing passenger business.

There can be no question of the great importance of this
new line to the capital of the nation; it secures uninterrupted communication with, and facilities to and from,
points never heretofore enjoyed by us, and the tendency will
inevitably be to draw more attention to Washington and
vicinity as the great political, social, and manufacturing
center of the country, and its growth must be rapid. With
the establishment here of repair and workshops of this enterprising company a large accession of excellent citizens—
skilled workmen in wood and metals—will be made. The
happiness, security, and comfort of this class of citizens it
should be a prime object of the Legislative Assembly to
insure by wise and careful legislation.

The Chesapeake and Ohio railroad, now completed to
Catletsburg, at the mouth of the Big Sandy river, 150

miles above Cincinnati, and 350 miles below Pittsburg on the Ohio river, is an additional and highly important link in the chain of communication with the far West.

At present we connect with this road only by way of the Orange and Alexandria railway at Charlottesville; but ere long we are to•have a more direct line by way of the Piedmont and Potomac railway, which starts from Washington and, doubtless, *via* the line of the Aqueduct road, and crossing the Potomac at the Great Falls, and thence on, *via* Aldie, to Staunton, Va., thereby shortening the route to Staunton thirty miles.

This connection with the Chesapeake and Ohio railroad will give us the shortest communication with the West and Southwest, making the most direct line between St. Louis and New York, the distance saved being estimated at not less than 140 miles. It will also connect us with that great system of railroads reaching the Pacific ocean, of which the Chesapeake and Ohio railroad will be the eastern terminus at Staunton, or rather by the Piedmont and Potomac road, *via* the Great Falls, at Washington.

The country with which we shall be brought into communication by the Piedmont and Potomac railroad is one of surpassing fertility. It is to traverse the counties of Loudon, Fauquier, Rappahannock, Page, Rockingham, and Augusta, (in Virginia,) all within the rich blue grass rigion of that State.

On its line are to be found coal in abundance and iron in immense quantities and of rare quality: marble not more than thirty miles distant from Washington, and within fifteen miles of the Great Falls, equal to that imported from Italy, at a large profit: while salt, lead, gypsum, lime, and petroleum abound on the lines with which it connects. This, making both the national capital and the Great Falls important points on the shortest line of travel

from Cincinnati and St. Louis to the North, will lead to
a large increase of population and wealth at both of these
points, which has hitherto avoided us because of the re-
puted greater cost of living—an objection now exploded.

This company proposes large expenditures in our city,
as its workshops, foundry, and car'works are to be located
here, and it is, in short, to be a Washington institution.

The Alexandria and Fredericksburg railroad will bring
to us, as purchasers, the residents of the peninsula south
of us in Maryland ; and the Point of Rocks railroad, which
will eventually connect by branch or cross-road with the
Great Falls, will open to us for competition with Baltimore the trade of those counties of Maryland north of us.

The Washington and Point Lookout railway opens the
whole region of Maryland between the Potomac and
Chesapeake Bay to our manufacturers and merchants, and
afford us easy connection with one of the most healthful
and beautiful regions of the State of Maryland. And by
our several lines of railway we directly reach the iron
supply in Tennessee, Kentucky, Virginia, Pennsylvania,
and Maryland, the abundant and fine wood of Virginia,
and all the corn and wheat, cattle, and farm produce for
home use and for commerce, while, by the deep and broad
river and the Chesapeake and Ohio canal, we may bring
to the Great Falls every article of foreign production.

In addition to these railroads there are divers other
lines about to, and, sooner or later, inevitably will, be constructed, which will greatly favor our projected development of the vast WATER POWER of the Potomac, and especially at the GREAT FALLS, where we are determined to
found, build, and populate a city commensurate with the
spirit of the times.

It is now understood that the Baltimore and Ohio Railroad Company are proceeding to build a railway from Laurel, on the Washington branch of their road, *via* Rockville, and thence across the Potomac, (and probably,) at the Great Falls, through the Blue Ridge, *via* Snickers Gap, connecting with their line extending from Harper's Ferry, *via* Winchester, down the Shenandoah valley. And, in order to compete with the line of the Piedmont and Potomac and Chesapeake and Ohio railroads, which form the most direct line West yet established, they will doubtless continue the direct line from Laurel, *via* Snicker's Gap, on to Grafton or Flemington, or some other air-line point of the western branch of the Baltimore and Ohio railway, whereby they can still shorten the route *via* Cincinnati to St. Louis over 100 miles.

COAL.

Coal being one of the chief factors of the manufacturing interest, it is important that we consider the supply in our vicinity and convenient reach. Thus far it is equal to the demand; but when new channels shall have been opened for transportation, and larger consumption required, the product may be increased in an immensely enlarged ratio. We give below a table showing the product for a series of years of the Cumberland coal region. This properly belongs to the great Allegheny coal field, and includes the Frostburg basin, about five miles wide and thirty miles long, (giving an area of 150 square miles,) and that lying between the Savage mountain and Negro mountain, containing about 130 square miles, and the trough or basin of the Youghiogheny, between Negro mountain and Laurel hill, containing about 250 square miles, making a total area of this coal field in Maryland about 550 square miles. The coal of this region is, taken to market, in Washington, by the Chesapeake and Ohio canal, or to Baltimore by the Baltimore and Ohio railroad. The following is the table referred to:

Year.	Tonnage by railroad.	Tonnage by canal.	Total.
1842	1,708		1,708
1845	24,653		24,653
1850	192,806	3,042	196,848
1855	478,486	183,786	662,272
1860	493,031	283,249	788,909
1864	377,684	260,368	636,236
1865	500,293	340,736	903,495
1866	736,153	341,160	1,079,331
1867	735,669	458,009	1,193,822
1868	848,118	484,849	1,330,443
1869	1,230,518	661,828	1,882,669
1870	1,112,938	606,707	1,717,075
1871	1,494,814	850,339	2,345,153
1872	1,866,699	1,093,971	2,973,233

NOTE.—These amounts have sometimes included the coal used on or along the railroad.

This coal was afforded in our markets, in 1850, at retail, for consumption, at $5 per ton, and, in 1871, at $6 for the lump. The cost by the quantity, according to the statement of large consumers in our city, iron-founders, machinists, and the like, has averaged, for years to the present time, at the wharf, from $3 50 to $4 25 per ton. At this writing, we are informed, it is about $4 per ton. In addition to all this supply, which is almost at our own hands, the quick communication by railroad, via Gordonsville, with the vast coal fields in the New River and Kanawha valleys of West Virginia, will bring to our wharves and workshops any amount of the splint and cannel coals. It is estimated that the coal territory in these valleys have an extent of over 600 square miles. This is wider than the fields which supply the vast industries and commerce of Great Britain—demands which amount to more than 100,000,000 tons annually. The great bituminous coal basin of the geologists, extending northward to the head-waters of the Hockhocking river, near Columbus, Ohio, southeast to the Peak of Otter, in Virginia, northeast to the middle of western Pennsylvania, and southwest to the Muscle Shoal, in northern Alabama, irregular in its entire length, 800 miles, and width from 30 to 180 miles, covers an area of 55,000 square miles, of which 1,800, contained in Virginia, hold the great center with respect to quantity and quality, whether cannel, splint, or bituminous coal. The Kanawha river runs through these beds, and so does the (yet unfinished) Chesapeake and Ohio railroad; so also, it may be said, does every road or stream in West Virginia. In one place, we are informed, the Chesapeake and Ohio railroad cuts an eleven-foot vein. The Virginia coal used, by estimate, would yield 45,000 tons per acre, or 28,800,000 tons per square mile.

It is more easily mined than other coal, because of the prodigious thickness of the veins, (from three to fifteen feet,) their horizontal position, and the comparative absence of noxious gases and volatile fumes. No shaft mining, machine lifting, pumping, or the like are necessary in working them.

With regard to quality the Virginia coal beds are "fat." That they are superior has been demonstrated by experience, but more nicely by accurate analysis. One of the results is here noted: The amount of ash residue left upon analysis amounts to but two per cent. The only other coal approaching this was the Snow-shoe coal of Pennsylvania, of limited supply, which gave 2.07 per cent. Other approved coal showed the true contrast. For example: The Phillipsburg yielded 10 per cent.; Frostburg, 11 per cent.; and the Maryland Company coal, 15.82 per cent., or nearly eight times that of the Kanawha coal.

As to uses, the splint coal, nowhere so abundant as in Virginia, is known to surpass any other for smelting ores, particularly iron ore. The uses of bituminous coal for manufacturing gas, driving machinery, and for fuel need no illustration. Cannel coal, besides its other uses, is likely to supplant wells as a source of petroleum. The Kanawha yields sixty-four gallons of crude oil per ton, equal to 1,260,000 gallons per acre.

The fact is seldom adverted to that, from the deficiency of shorter water transportation, great quantities of the Kanawha coal is boated to New Orleans, and thence tran-shipped by sea all the way to New York.

The two great factors in building up a manufacturing town are coal and iron. We have already shown that scarcely a point now known in the world has more admir-able locations relative to a vast supply of coal, easy means of access, and water transportation for commerce, than the city of Washington; and what is, or can be, said in this respect as to Washington must soon apply to the Great Falls; and as these different classes of coal are so near at hand, available in such immense quantities, and can be so readily brought to this market, it is evident that, for every purpose of commerce, for manufacturing or domestic use, they can be afforded in more abundant supply and at lower prices than at any place along the coast, or at any other point available for water shipment.

The supply and consumption of the several kinds of coal in the United States and the amount exported therefrom annually, sums up per year, for the last two years, about as follows:

Anthracite sent to market, (official)	14,965,501
Consumed in the coal regions (estimated)	2,720,000
Bituminous sent toward seaboard, including 443,955 tons imported, (official)	4,895,914
Bituminous mined and consumed in the United States, (estimated)	11,500,000
	34,081,415
Exported	269,751
Total supply for United States	33,811,664

This would exhaust one square mile, or, in other words, one-eighteen-thousandth of the Virginia coal beds per annum. This much for quantity.

IRON.

This indispensible article lies in considerable quantities at and around the Great Falls, but when you cross the Blue Ridge and strike the Shenandoah river along through Warren, Page, Rockingham, and other counties, it is to be found in abundance, and of a superior quality; and along parallel 39, the probable route of the next air-line railway to St. Louis, it is still more abundant.

The New river, rising in North Carolina, becomes the Kanawha after crossing the Alleghenies, and receiving the Greenbrier river in the neighborhood of the White Sulpher. Above that region coal diminishes and iron increases. New river might be called an iron-clad stream. Giles, Bland, Pulaski, and Grayson are among the richest iron counties, though crossing to the waters of Tennessee (Clinch and Holston rivers) the mountains are everywhere affluent with ore, not always without coal for utilizing it. As Horace Greeley remarked in an article which appeared in *The Tribune* (October 21, 1871,) on this general subject: "In most counties of either Virginia, excellent coal or ore (often both in close proximity) can now be bought at prices ranging from $5 to $15 per acre. Many of the acres have a rich, deep virgin soil, with a splendid growth of forest trees covering two-thirds to three-fourths of them—lands which, in Pennsylvania, would be deemed dirt-cheap at $1,000 per acre. Who can doubt that free labor with railroads will soon give a like value to the mineral lands of old and West Virginia?" And we may here call attention to the fact that the iron ores of Virginia and West Virginia are considered among the best in the world, and are found in unlimited quantities upon the immediate line of railroad communication with most unusual facilities for their profitable working. The coal and iron accessible are estimated to exceed in quality and amount those of the whole of Great Britain, and with this special advantage, that, unlike those of that country, they are found near the surface of the earth and can be readily mined. In our sources of supply the expense of production is, as near as possible, the minimum, from the very case from which the material is dug and laid down at the point of shipment. In Great Britain it is estimated that there is invested in pits and machinery a capital amounting to upward of $200,000,000, and all practically dead capital. In these mines the laws of gravity furnish easy drainage, ventilation, and carriage.

By a circular put forth in the Kanawha iron region, which has recently fallen under our notice, we learn that a ton of iron can be there produced for $15. Now, as coal can be laid down here at from $4 to $4 50 per ton, and the ore at a similar low figure, it is demonstrable that iron can be produced here at from $20 to $25 per ton, and thus laid down, as it were, in a market where it readily brings from $50 to $55 per ton to-day.

CLIMATICS, ETC.

As of incalculable importance, in view of building up a manufacturing city, we would call attention to the climate and the circumstances affecting the health of a population. With but a single exception it is proven that the country about Washington is among the most healthful sections of America, and that exception is malaria, which, along the lower water of the Potomac, has been somewhat troublesome, but which at Washington is no longer prevalent, and at the Great Falls almost, and will entirely, disappear with the vigorous growth of a well-drained, ventilated city.

What we quote in this connection, from the report previously referred to, relative to the District of Columbia, has, in every particular, increased advantages when applied to the region of the Great Falls as being more elevated, more undulating, and abundantly supplied with springs of pure, cool water.

The best test in this regard is that of facts. We present here a table of the death rate of this city, compared with that of the few cities whence data of any reliability can be procured:

The death rate of	Washington, per 1,000, averages		20
"	"	Philadelphia, " "	22
"	"	New York, " "	28
"	"	Boston, " "	23
"	"	St. Louis, " "	27
"	"	Cincinnati, " "	26
"	"	Chicago, " "	25

There is yet another very important fact to which we may quite pertinently refer here, and that is the almost total immunity of Washington from epidemic diseases. Never but once has it suffered at all, and then (during the cholera visitation of 1832) it is well known that the disease was not only less general, but was much less virulent, than in any other city in the country.

Not to attempt a scientific dissertation on the probable causes of this immunity and the general healthiness of this city, we will advert to only two of them, namely, the complete ventilation by our wide streets and avenues, and the remarkable purity of our water supply. A distinguished writer recently said: "The evil consequences of an impure supply" (and we may add, per contra, the blessings of an abundant supply,) "of pure water, is deserving of the most serious consideration." Scientific investigation has shown that the health of communities cannot possibly be assured where the water supplied for drinking purposes is impure. So true is this that carefully prepared estimates, made during the prevalence of an epidemic, show that in the city of London, which is supplied with water procured from different sources, the rate of mortality increased in the different sections of the city in direct ratio to the degree of impurity of the water supplied to them. For instance, in London, in 1854, the water supplied by the Lambeth Company was very free from contamination, while that supplied by the Southwark Company contained much sewage. Both companies had pipes laid in the same streets, and the water was supplied indiscriminately. Among those who used the Southwark water, the deaths amounted to 130 in 10,000, and 2,500 persons were destroyed by it in one season. Among those who used the Lambeth water, the deaths amounted to only 37 in 10,000.

As to the impurities of which we speak. it should be stated that we refer to the presence of organic matter, and not to the calcium and magnesium salts, for instance, which, within certain limits, are considered innocuous. It has been incontrovertibly affirmed, after the most searching investigation, that multitudes of diseases whose causes were long considered occult, owe their origin to the presence of impurities in the water used for drinking purposes. In view of these facts, then. it can hardly be questioned that we are largely indebted to the very pure water with which we are supplied for the high sanitary condition of the city.

We give below a tabular statement showing the quality of our own water supply as compared with that of some others. All but the estimate of the Potomac water we copy from Professor C. F. Chandler's lecture on water, delivered before the American Institute of New York :

City.	Source.	Organic and volatile matter.
Washington.........	Washington supply...........	0.54
New York...........	Croton average for thirteen weeks in 1867.	0.66
New York...........	Croton average for three months in 1868.	1.14
New York...........	Croton average for six months in 1869...	0.67
New York	Well west of Central Park	1.55
Brooklyn	Ridgewood	0.59
Boston	Cochituate, (E. N. Horsford).............	0.71
Philadelphia	Fairmount	1.20
Philadelphia	Delaware.........	0.55
Albany	Hydrant..	2.31
Troy.........	Hydrant.........	1.34
Utica.........	Hydrant.........	0.96
Syracuse...........	New reservoir	1.80
Cleveland...........	Lake Erie.........	1.53
Chicago	Lake Michigan.........	1.06
Rochester............	Genesee river.........	1.23
Schenectady	State street well	2.33
Newark .... ⎫		
Jersey City........ ⎬		
Hoboken.........	Passaic river.........	2.86
Hudson City..... ⎭		
Trenton	Delaware river.........	0.55
London.............	Thames	0.83
Dublin...............	Lough Vartry	1.34
Paris	Seine	1.00
Amsterdam..........	River Vecht.........	2.13

NOTE.—The above estimates are calculated for one gallon of 231 cubic inches.

Next as to the influence of temperature upon labor, we give here a table showing the temperature of Washington beside that of other cities, first giving an exhibit, furnished by the courtesy of the Chief Signal Officer of the Army, of the mean temperature of the District of Columbia, for winter, spring, summer, and autumn since 1860:

Months.	Temperature.	Months.	Temperature.	Months.	Temperature.	Months.	Temperature.
December...	35.4	March	41.5	June	70.9	September..	68.3
January.....	32.8	April.........	52.1	July	75.5	October	55.6
February ...	34.7	May	63.4	August.....	74.3	November..	45.4
Winter.....	34.3	*Spring*......	52.3	*Summer*....	73.6	*Autumn*.....	56.4

This gives us a mean temperature of 54.15°, which varies from Blodgett's isothermal charts by only 0.85°.

Now, with reference to extremes of temperature, of which much has been ignorantly said to the prejudice of Washington, we collate from Blodgett's work reports of observations, as follows:

	Years.
New Bedford, from 1812 to 1856	44
New York City, from 1822 to 1854	32
Albany, New York, from 1826 to 1854	28
Philadelphia, from 1798 to 1856	58
Washington and Baltimore, from 1817 to 1855	38
Cincinnati, from 1835 to 1854	19
St. Louis, from 1833 to 1855	22

Extremes of temperature.

	January.	February.	March.	April.	May.	June.	July.	August.	September.	October.	November.	December.
New Bedford	49	49	58	67	77	86	87	84	81	71	61	51
	7	3	12	26	37	46	54	52	41	30	20	7
New York City	49	59	62	72	82	89	93	89	85	73	62	50
	7	9	18	31	41	52	60	60	47	35	24	14
Albany, New York	48	48	51	76	84	89	92	88	84	71	61	48
	-8	-5	7	23	36	48	55	50	39	27	17	-1
Philadelphia	56	55	68	78	85	91	93	89	87	76	68	56
	8	9	17	28	44	50	60	57	45	34	24	14
Wash. and Baltimore	56	59	69	79	85	91	94	91	88	77	67	56
	9	12	20	32	43	53	61	59	46	33	24	16
Cincinnati	62	64	76	87	90	94	95	93	91	81	71	61
	3	4	15	27	39	49	57	55	41	28	18	8
St. Louis	61	65	75	86	99	95	9	95	92	82	71	60
	4	1	16	31	41	51	58	57	45	25	18	7

NOTE.—In the above table the upper line of figures represents the maximum and the lower the minimum temperature of each city in degrees of Fahrenheit

The presentation of this table, the result of many years'

careful scientific observation, ought to be enough to satisfy
the most skeptical mind.

A glance at the figures will show that the temperature
of Washington and Philadelphia are almost identical,
while it is interesting to compare their extremes of temperature with those of St. Louis and Cincinnati.
The maximum and minimum temperature of the two
cities of Philadelphia and Washington differ, as follows:

	Jan.	Feb.	Mar.	April.	May.	June.	July.	Aug.	Sept.	Oct.	Nov.	Dec.
Maximum.......	==	1†	1†	1†	==	==	1†	2†	1†	1†	1—	==
Minimum......	1†	3†	3†	1†	1—	3†	1†	2†	1†	1 ·	==	2†

NOTE.—Here the sign == shows when they are coincident, † when
the Washington temperature exceeds, and — when it is less than that
of Philadelphia.

It will be seen that what little difference there is (though
there is practically none) in the matter of extremes, is in
favor of Washington—the extremes are less.

If there is any truth in the statement that Washington
is an unfavorable place to live in for manufacturing purposes, it must apply with equal force to Philadelphia, and
greater to St. Louis and Cincinnati. By far the greater
number of our best citizens engaged in mechanical and
industrial enterprises have spent much time in the same
avocations in Northern cities, and we have their testimony, that can be relied on, that Washington is far pref-
erable in this respect to many of the Northern cities.

But to those who deem the extreme summer heats of this
latitude as unfavorable to labor, we would say that the
days are few in which men, white and black, may not be
found pursuing their avocations, without inconvenience,

in the sun. But the point is: That, taking the year *as a whole*, there are more available days here for comfortable labor than can be found in any portion of New England or New York—the great manufacturing hives of the continent. In fact, the months from September to January, and from February to May, a great portion of which are cold, wet, stormy, and uncomfortable in the sections named, are here the most genial and healthful of the whole year. The testimony of manufacturers and laborers taken before this committee were clear on the point that, taking the year through, a man can labor more days in the year in this latitude than in that of any of the principal towns of New England.

We have thus, even at the risk of seeming prolix, passed in review the history of this locality, with its past and prospective advantages, as bearing on the question before us.

An invaluable auxiliary to the healthfulness of a growing city, and more especially a manufacturing city, is the quantity, quality, and cost of food, and in this connection we quote from the foregoing mentioned report to show some advantages of this locality.

The supply of abundant and excellent food for any population we may have here for years to come cannot but be abundant. Consider this region, of so great an extent, so admirably adapted to agriculture! The farming land within an easy day's journey hence, in any direction, has scarcely begun to be developed, so that we set at rest any speculation or doubt as to whither will come food for a future population, though largely increased. It is within our memory, that, during the troubled times of the war, for many years the rich Shenandoah and Kanawha valleys were the best sources of supplies of food and cattle for the Virginia armies. If these hosts could be fed in the turmoil of war and strife, when labor and production were at a standstill, it is easy to see that the inducement of fair compensation would increase the past supply immensely. Even before the war these regions were a noted source of supply of fine cattle to the markets of Baltimore and Philadelphia.

In another connection we have spoken of the capacity of this section of country for wool-growing, and here refer to the additional facility for supplying mutton—the most healthful and cheapest article of animal food. But for vegetables, cereals, and fruits, we claim that Virginia cannot be excelled. Apples, pears, and peaches are nowhere more abundant, or of better quality; and grapes grow wild all over this region in great abundance, and in quality equal to the best varieties in our markets. Thus affording at home articles of luxury, as well as staple, for our tables. And while referring to the supply afforded by this section of beef and mutton for the markets, it is not irrelevant to mention that it is also famous—especially the counties of Loudon and Farquier—for its fine-blooded horses, as well as its fine stock of draught animals—both horses and mules. All these considerations we deem of vital importance as concomitants to the growth and prosperity of a manufacturing city.

SCHOOLS IN WASHINGTON.

We quote in regard to schools to show the spirit which prevails in regard to popular education, the great improvements made and the determination of the people to attain to a system of public schools not inferior to any in the United States; and to accomplish which, talent, experience, and precedent have been borrowed from every State

3 G F

of the Union, and the best results from all have attempted
to be copied:

The white population of Washington in 1870 was......... 73,744
" colored   "   "   "   "   "   35,455

Total......... 109,199

White children, between 6 and 17 years of age, in Washington
was... 17,403
Colored children, between 6 and 17 years of age, in Washington
was.. 8,532

Total...... 25,935

From 1802 to 1840 very little was done for public free-
schools in Washington. During that period there was
never more than five hundred children received into what
was called public schools, and on an average not more
than three hundred. All the free-schools were then considered schools for poor children, and were never popular.
In 1840 there were but two schools, one in the western
the other in the eastern district. The whole number of
pupils received into both was four hundred and thirty-
two, and the average only two hundred and ninety-six.
The whole cost of both schools was but $1,500.

In 1850 the schools had increased in number to fourteen,
which were taught by fourteen principals and five assistants. The whole number of pupils received was 1,339,
while the cost amounted to $7,685 88.

At the close of the next decade (1860) the number of
schools had increased to fifty with fifty teachers.

The number of pupils enrolled amounted to 4,296, and
the cost was $29,821. At this period there were no pub-
lic, and only three or four private schools for colored
children in the city. · But mark the change and progress
in the next ten years.

In 1870 the number of white schools was one hundred

and seventeen ; principal teachers, one hundred and seventeen; assistants, six; music teachers, two; and German teachers, two ; in all, one hundred and twenty-seven.

- The whole number or pupils enrolled was 10,753.

The cost for the white schools, aside from new buildings and
improvements, was... $173,250
New buildings and improvements.. 73,500

Giving, for white schools, a total expenditure of................... $246,750

In 1870 the number of colored schools was fifty-eight, with fifty-eight teachers.

The number of pupils enrolled was 6,681, which, added to the number of white children, (10,753,) gives a total of 17,434 pupils enrolled.

The whole cost of the colored schools, aside from new build-
ings, &c., amounted to.. $83,367
Add total for white children.. 246,750

And we have a total expenditure of....................................... $330,117

In Georgetown and the county the change is no less marked. The private and charity schools of Washington received, in 1870, 6,309, and those of Georgetown, 1,000 pupils. Thus, 23.743 out of the 25,935 children of school age have been enrolled in public or private schools. The work is still progressing, and larger, more commodious and beautiful school buildings are now being erected than we have seen in any city which it has recently been our good fortune to visit.

With churches it is the same. More than ninety different houses dedicated to the worship of God are found in the District, where all may worship, with "none to molest or make afraid."

Again, there is scarcely a locality where the education of the rising generation is exciting more general interest. The population which we invite may count upon every advantage in this respect for their children.

We are indebted to Mr. Z. Richards—so long a valuable teacher in, and now Auditor of the District—for the foregoing facts.

With regard to new private improvements in the District of Columbia, there has been $3,421,265 worth erected within the last year, (1872,) nearly all of which are of the most comfortable and substantial dwellings and business edifices, with modern improvements, and adapted to every grade of society. And, happily, our population is correspondingly increasing. In short, the spirit of improvements is thoroughly at work in this District, and necessarily alive to, and, in self-interest, will most earnestly coöperate with any corresponding measures for surrounding or neighboring improvements.

www.ingramcontent.com/pod-product-compliance
Lightning Source LLC
Chambersburg PA
CBHW020818030726
47496CB00009B/2945

* 9 7 8 3 3 3 7 2 3 9 0 7 7 *